The Puppy Who Couldn't Sleep

The Puppy Who Couldn't Sleep

by Holly Webb
Illustrated by Sophy Williams

tiger tales

tiger tales

5 River Road, Suite 128, Wilton, CT 06897
Published in the United States 2020
Originally published in Great Britain 2019
by the Little Tiger Group
Text copyright © 2019 Holly Webb
Illustrations copyright © 2019 Sophy Williams
Author photograph © Charlotte Knee Photography
ISBN-13: 978-1-68010-457-8
ISBN-10: 1-68010-457-8
Printed in China
STP/1800/0286/1019
All rights reserved
10 9 8 7 6 5 4 3 2 1

For more insight and activities, visit us at www.tigertalesbooks.com

Contents

For George

This book was inspired by a true story about a dog in a rescue center who couldn't sleep unless he was in a cardboard box. Rescue centers are amazing places, staffed by wonderful people. If your local cat or dog rescue has a fundraising event, please consider going to it!

Chapter One
Oliver's Discovery

"So you've definitely done all your homework for tomorrow?" Lara's dad glanced down at her as they turned the corner into their road. "I need to remember to fill out that form about your field trip to the museum."

Lara sighed. "Yes, Dad. I even looked at the spelling words. But did you have to mention homework?

Now I've got that Sunday afternoon feeling...."

"I'm sorry." Dad put his arm around Lara's shoulders. "I think Oliver's got it, too. He loves it when it's the weekend and he gets long walks with both of us." The big greyhound cross glanced up when he heard his name, clearly wondering why Lara and her dad were talking about him. He

8

wafted his long, sandy tail once, but that was all. He'd been racing around in the grass with Lara, and he was very tired. He was anxious to get home to flop in his basket.

"Can I make a smoothie later?" Lara asked her dad hopefully. She knew there were some bananas going mushy at the bottom of the fruit bowl, but the last time she'd made one, it had somehow exploded out of the blender.

"Ummm...," Dad began. "Hey, Oliver! This way." He tugged gently on Oliver's leash. The greyhound cross had stopped and was staring down a little alley, a few houses from where they lived. He looked at Dad when he felt the pull of the leash, but he didn't move.

"Can you smell something good down there?" Lara asked, sniffing. Oliver was a really well-behaved dog most of the time, but he loved food and didn't care if it had fallen out of a garbage can. Or even if it was still in a garbage can.... "Did someone drop some fries again, Oliver? Is it fries?"

"Don't encourage him!" Dad said, rolling his eyes. Fries were one of Oliver's favorite things, and he knew the word. Usually saying "fries" would have him leaping around and wagging his tail so hard that it looked like it would fall off.

But the greyhound cross didn't seem to have noticed. He was still staring into the alley, and now he tugged harder on his leash.

"Come on, Oliver," Lara said in a coaxing voice. "Oliver! Time to go home."

"I wonder if there's a fox or something by those garbage cans," Dad said thoughtfully. "He really wants to go down there. Though he's never been that excited about foxes before."

Oliver was a big dog, big enough that he could stand upright with his paws on Dad's shoulders if he wanted to. If he didn't want to walk, it was hard to make him.

"Come on, boy," Dad said. "I don't want to pull you home. What is it?"

Oliver tugged on the leash again, and this time Dad let him pace slowly down the alley, toward the broken-down fence at the end. The alley ran down the side of the convenience store and then along the back of a little row of shops. It was where the shop's garbage cans were, and all the vans drove down it to unload boxes. It always looked a little messy.

Lara wrinkled her nose at the smell from the garbage cans and hoped she wouldn't see any rats. Her friend Amelia had pet rats named Timmy and Trouble, and Lara loved to play with them, but rats that lived around garbage cans weren't the same thing at all. Maybe it was a rat that Oliver could smell?

Something moved behind the garbage cans, and Lara swallowed a squeak of fright.

"Lara, go back," Dad said. "If it's a fox, it might snap. I don't want you anywhere near it."

"It isn't a fox, Dad," Lara said, pointing. "Look."

Peering around a big garbage can was a small black nose, followed by the rest of a skinny little black dog.

13

"A dog!" Dad said, sounding surprised. "Hey, puppy. Where did you come from?"

The dog darted back behind the garbage cans as soon as he heard Dad's voice, and Dad shook his head. "I scared him. Poor little thing."

"Did Oliver smell him all the way from the other end of the alley?" Lara whispered.

"He must have. You're a clever old thing, Oliver, aren't you?" Dad patted his head. "Did you see if he had a collar, Lara? He must be lost—unless he's a stray, of course."

"I don't think so." Lara watched as the small black head appeared around the side of the garbage can again. "What are we going to do?" The dog was obviously scared—he was hunched over with his ears laid flat against the back of his head, and he was shivering. Lara couldn't tell if it was Oliver he was scared of, or her and Dad. Oliver wasn't showing his teeth or anything like that; he just looked interested.

"I guess we should take him to a dog rescue," Dad said, but he didn't sound very sure. "Or maybe the vet, to see if he's microchipped? I don't know if any of them will be open on a Sunday afternoon, though."

"So … we need to catch him?" Lara asked, keeping her voice low.

"Yeah…." Dad rubbed his chin. "But I'm not sure how we're going to do that. I mean we're what, 15 feet away? And he's already so nervous. I'm starting to think he must be a stray, because he doesn't seem very used to people."

The black puppy was huddled against the side of the garbage can, as though he was too frightened to move, and Lara felt guilty. It was horrible that they were upsetting the little dog. But it would be even worse to leave him there all on his own.

Dad edged a little closer and Oliver went with him, crouching down with his front paws out in a bow and putting his head to one side to show he was friendly. But the puppy didn't seem to understand. He pressed himself back against the garbage can, whining, and then suddenly he took off. He dashed along the fence and through a tiny gap where the wooden slats had rotted.

"Oh, no." Dad sighed. "I don't think we have a chance of finding him now."

Lara frowned, standing on tiptoe to try and peer over the fence. "What's behind it? I can't figure it out."

"It's the industrial park—you know,

those buildings we go past on the way to school, where the gym is? There's a bunch of brambles and bushes just beyond the fence. I bet that's where he's hiding."

Lara knew Dad was right. They'd never be able to find the little dog now—not unless he wanted to be found.

"Come on, Oliver." Dad turned to head for home, and the big greyhound followed him reluctantly, still watching the fence as if he hoped the other dog would come back.

"What are we going to do, Dad?" Lara asked anxiously. "We can't just leave him there."

"I know. It's tricky," Dad admitted. "But we'll think of something. Don't worry." He put his arm around Lara's shoulders, and they walked slowly along the alley to the road.

The black puppy crept back to the fence and watched them go, his tail beating uncertainly from side to side. The big dog was looking behind him, and the puppy took a step toward the hole, wondering if he should follow. But then they vanished around the corner. The puppy stood watching the far end of the alley for a moment, his tail still flickering. Then he crept through the hole and slunk back to the pile of old cardboard boxes that someone had dumped by the garbage cans. He crawled inside a half-squashed box and curled himself up tight.

Chapter Two
Wanting to Help

Lara hung up Oliver's leash on its hook by the front door. Then she pushed her glasses higher up her nose and looked anxiously at Dad. "We have to do something about the puppy. He was so little and thin. And really scared."

"I know." Dad nodded. "I'm going to put the kettle on and then I'll call the animal rescue center—maybe they can help. They might be able to send someone out to pick him up. The staff there will take care of him, and if someone's trying to find him, they can get him from the rescue center. I'll look up the number now." Dad filled up the kettle, then got out his phone and started searching for the rescue center's website.

Lara watched him hopefully as he called, but then he made a face at her. "It's just a recorded message—they're closed. Oh, hang on! Please pass me a pen." Lara grabbed one off the table, and Dad scribbled down a phone number on the edge of his newspaper.

"Whose number is that?" Lara asked as he hung up.

"The town's animal control. The

21

recorded message said to call them if you found a lost dog. I don't know if they'll be answering the phone this late on a Sunday afternoon, though. Let's see." He tapped in the number.

Lara watched him worriedly, biting her bottom lip.

"It'll be okay," Dad whispered as it started to ring. "Oh. Answering machine. Yes, hi. This is Dave Fisher. I've just found a dog in an alley behind the stores on Lakeview Road. It looked like a puppy, and very

22

thin, too, so I'm not sure if it's been there a while. We couldn't get anywhere near him. I'm not sure how this works, whether you come out to find him. Anyway, here's my number if you want me to show you where he was." Lara's dad recited his cell phone number and ended the call. Then he sighed. "Well, hopefully they'll call us back."

"But no one's going to do anything now," Lara said, frowning.

"No," Dad admitted. "I expect it'll be tomorrow morning."

"Do you think we should go out and look for him again?" Lara suggested.

Dad was silent for a moment, and then he slipped the phone into his pocket and gave her a hug. "I'm not sure it's going to do any good, sweetheart. The little dog was really scared. I don't think we'll be able to get close enough to catch him. It's probably best left to someone who knows what they're doing—like animal control." He crouched down to look at Lara in the eye. "I'm worried about the puppy, too," he said gently. Then he laughed as Oliver came nosing in between them and licked Lara's cheek. "And so is Oliver."

Lara smiled sadly, wiping the wet dog lick off her cheek and rubbing Oliver's ear. His dark eyes really did look anxious.

"I promise we won't just forget about him," Dad said. "I'll call animal control again tomorrow and ask what they're going to do." He glanced down at his watch. "It's almost seven, and we haven't even had dinner! Come on—you can help me get it ready."

Lara nodded. She hadn't realized she was hungry until her dad had mentioned dinner. But when the pasta was cooked and she'd grated some cheese to put on top, she ended up pushing most of it from one side of her plate to the other.

"Lost your appetite?" Dad asked.

Lara sighed. "No. It's just…. I keep thinking how skinny the puppy was."

Her dad put down his fork. "I know. Well, don't eat it if you really don't want to. But you'll probably wake up in the middle of the night feeling hungry. At least have a banana."

Lara didn't feel like eating, but Dad was right, so she nibbled the banana in tiny bites while he finished his pasta. "Can I call Mom?" she asked.

"Sure," Dad said. "Ask her if she has any ideas about how we can catch the puppy—you know she's really good with dogs." Lara's mom and dad had split up when she was little, and Lara's mom lived a long way away with her new husband, Jake, and Lara's sister, Kelly. Lara went to stay with them during school vacations, and she loved getting to play with Kelly and their two golden retrievers. "Not for too long though, love," he added. "It's definitely bedtime."

Lara nodded. She decided to get ready for bed first and then call her mom from her room.

Oliver followed her upstairs and slumped down on the big cushion next to Lara's bed, so she sat next to him on the floor and rubbed his ears while she waited for her mom to answer.

"Hello, Lara! Is everything all right?" Her mom sounded a little worried—it was later than Lara would usually call.

"Yeah. It's just … we found a stray dog, and it's really sad."

"Oh, no—is the dog okay?"

"I don't know. He ran off before we could get a good look at him. Dad called animal control, but it was just a recorded message. He says they'll probably come and look for the dog tomorrow. He wondered if you can think of anything else we might do to catch him. He's only a puppy, Mom, and I think he's out there all on his own." Lara sniffed. Telling her mom about the dog was making her feel worse, not better.

"Oh, wow, I don't know." Her mom was silent for a minute. "I guess you could put some food out, but to be honest, it's probably better if you leave it to animal control, Lara. They'll know how to do it without scaring him."

"But … what happens after that?" Lara whispered.

"They'll take him to the rescue center. Probably that one near you. Valley Animal Care. He'll be taken care of really well. The people who work at animal rescues are amazing."

"I guess…." Lara sighed. "Thanks, Mom, but I'd better go now. Dad said it was bedtime."

"Okay, love. Tell me if you find out anything more about the dog, please?"

"Yes." Lara sniffed again. "'Night." She got up to put the phone back in Dad's room and then went to sit next to Oliver again. He huffed sleepily at her and gave a comfortable sort of groan as she scratched the top of his head.

"You're such a lucky dog, do you know that?" Lara whispered to him. "You've got me and Dad, and we love you. We feed you a ton, even if we don't let you eat stuff that's fallen out of garbage cans when you want to. You've got this cushion and a basket downstairs…. I think Dad was right, and that puppy hasn't had a home for a while. He probably sleeps in those old cardboard boxes around the garbage cans in the alley. And I bet he's starving."

Oliver only snuffled at her in his sleep. Lara sighed, and then shivered a little. She pulled some of the comforter off her bed to wrap around her shoulders. Her window was open, and it was cold....

Farther down the street, the puppy gulped hungrily at a piece of old sandwich that had fallen out of the garbage can behind the convenience store. He was very hungry, so to get most of a sandwich was a treat, even if it was soggy from sitting in a puddle. He gobbled it down and sniffed around hopefully for anything else. Then his ears pricked up a little—there was a noise, someone moving around. He held still, pressing himself against the garbage can, and then he backed slowly toward the fence. It might be that dog again, and

the people with him. The dog had been very big, but he hadn't seemed fierce. The black puppy had been chased by other dogs before. He knew how to tell when they were friendly or not. Or he thought he did. He had been more scared of the people than the dog—the tall man towering over him like that. It had been better to run away. It always was.

The girl who worked at the convenience store locked the back door and hurried off down the alley, and the puppy let his twitching ears sag back. He was all alone again, and that was safe. But as he curled up inside his box, he shivered and huddled against the cardboard, remembering warm fur and milk and wriggling little bodies next to his.

Chapter Three
A Clever Plan

Lara told her best friend, Amelia, about the puppy the next day at school.

"I couldn't get to sleep forever," she whispered as Miss Okafor was taking attendance.

"Are you going to try finding him again?" Amelia whispered back.

Lara shook her head. "I don't know. Dad said that animal control would probably pick him up today, but I took a quick look down the alley this morning, and he wasn't there. I guess animal control will come while we're at school. They might even be looking for him now, and he'll be at the rescue center by the time I get home."

"That's good, isn't it?" Amelia asked. "They'll take care of him there."

"I know. It's just ... I wish I could take care of him." Lara blinked, surprised at herself. She hadn't realized that before. "I really wanted to help. He looked so scared. You're right, though. The rescue center is the best place for him."

But when Lara got home that afternoon, Dad told her that the puppy still hadn't been caught.

"Animal control couldn't find him," he explained. "She said she'd keep coming back, but that was all she could do."

"Oh...."

"She said the puppy has been spotted by the people who work in the nearby stores. He's been around there for a while, and no one has reported a small black puppy missing. So we'll keep an eye out for him when we're walking Oliver and on the way to school," Dad went on. "Then we can let animal control know if we see him. Maybe he's only there at certain times."

"Like in the evening?" Lara said thoughtfully, and she looked down the

36

road toward the alley.

"Maybe." Dad nodded. "She said they might be able to trap him once they know he's definitely there."

"Trap him?" Lara sounded worried. "That wouldn't hurt, would it?"

Her dad shook his head. "No. She said it's like a cage with a door that shuts once the dog is inside. It wouldn't hurt. Though I guess it would be a little scary."

Lara shivered, imagining it. She knew that animal control would only be trying to help, but the puppy had already looked so frightened. She hated the thought of him caught in a cage, not knowing what was going on.

Dad walked Lara to school the next morning with Oliver, but there was no sign of the little black dog. Oliver stopped to sniff at the entrance to the alley, but that was all. And it could have been because he could smell something delicious (or delicious according to him, at least).

"Have a good day." Dad hugged Lara good-bye at the gate. "You're walking home with Amelia this afternoon, right?"

"Uh-huh." The two girls sometimes walked home together on their own if they didn't have an after-school club.

"Okay. Make sure you watch the road carefully at the intersection."

"We will. 'Bye, Dad!" Lara waved to him and headed onto the playground, spotting Amelia over by the fence talking to a couple of their other friends.

"Any news?" Amelia asked hopefully, and Lara shook her head.

"Nope. Oliver didn't even act curiously today, so I don't think the puppy was there." She glanced eagerly at Amelia. "We could look for him on the way home this afternoon. Dad said that animal control would probably use a special trap to catch him. It sounds scary—I'd much rather we found him."

"Definitely!" Amelia agreed. "He sounds so sweet, the way you described him. I hope we see him."

Lara nodded. The puppy was cute. But if he'd gone away from the alley, maybe it was a good thing, because it would mean he'd found his way home. He'd seemed so scared and lost when they'd seen him before, though—Lara was almost sure he didn't have a home to go to.

"It's just along here," Lara said. "At the end of this row of stores."

"Oh, yeah." Amelia nodded. "I know

where you mean now. I'd forgotten this little alley was even here."

"I think it only gets used for delivering stuff to the stores," Lara explained. "It's really quiet most of the time, so it's the perfect place for him to hide. Are you sure you don't mind going down there? It's a little dirty. And there might be rats."

Amelia laughed. "I don't mind rats! I have two of them at home." But then she paused. "I know what you mean, though. It is pretty dirty. We'll just have to be careful and not touch anything. Hey!"

"What?" Lara spun around. "Did you see something?"

"I-I think so…." Amelia frowned. "Down at the end by those big garbage cans. Just a little face peering out."

"That's where we saw him before!" Lara caught hold of Amelia's hand, and they crept quietly down the alley, almost on tiptoe, until they were halfway between the garbage cans and the road.

"Yes, there!" Lara breathed. "It's him!" She tugged gently at Amelia as she saw the little dog looking at them. "Let's stop here. I think Dad and I scared him by going too close on Sunday." She crouched down and pulled off her backpack, digging out her lunch box. "Look, here's half my sandwich from lunch."

"Did you save that on purpose?" Amelia whispered, ducking down next to her.

"Yes.... Well, I was sort of hoping.... And it's ham—I thought he'd like that."

"I've got some cheese cubes I didn't have time to eat." Amelia took out her own lunch, making a rustling noise as she opened up the foil wrapped around the cheese.

43

"I think he heard you!" Lara's eyes widened. "Look, he's coming out a bit farther. Can you rustle the foil again?"

Amelia crinkled the foil with her fingers, and the girls glanced excitedly at each other as the little dog came out from between the garbage cans.

"He's so small!" Amelia said.

"I know. I hardly got a chance to look at him before. He's even thinner than I thought he was. Do you think we should throw him some pieces of food?"

"Maybe. Unless it scares him." Amelia sounded doubtful. She scrunched the foil again, and the puppy came a step closer. "Hold out some of your sandwich," she suggested.

Lara tore off a piece and slowly stretched out her arm. She laid the sandwich down on the pavement in front of her and looked hopefully at the dog.

The black puppy looked at Lara and Amelia, and then he looked at the sandwich. He seemed to be weighing it out—the food on one side, and the scary people on the other. He took another step forward and then made a sudden dash for the piece of sandwich, gulping it down in one mouthful before darting back again.

But he didn't go as far this time—just a few steps away.

"Try some of your cheese," Lara whispered, and Amelia pulled out one of the cubes of cheese. They both saw the puppy's tongue lick hopefully over his nose, and when Amelia put down the cheese just a little way from her feet, he came to gobble it up right away. Then he stood looking at the two girls, his tail slowly wagging, obviously waiting for more.

46

Slowly, carefully, Lara tore off another piece of sandwich, holding it out in the palm of her hand this time. She couldn't help giggling as the puppy took it, brushing his velvety muzzle against her hand. She longed to rub his flopped-over ears, but she was sure it would scare him away. "Should I give him the rest?" she whispered. "Or … do you think we could get him to follow us back to my house?"

Amelia caught her breath. "Would he?"

"He might. And that's got to be better than catching him in a trap, right? Oh!" Lara laughed, suddenly realizing that the puppy had gotten impatient while they were talking. He was right next to her now, poking his furry, whiskery

47

muzzle into her lunch box for more of her sandwich.

Very gently Lara ran her hand down his back and the puppy tensed up—she felt him go still all over. But then he relaxed again and went back to chasing the sandwich around her lunch box. "You can't eat that!" Lara gently pulled the plastic wrap out of his mouth. "It will make you sick." She petted him again, and this time, the puppy didn't seem to mind. He didn't tense up, and he glanced around curiously at Lara's hand, and licked her wrist.

"I think he might follow us," Amelia whispered. "I'm going to stand up."

She crinkled the foil and then stood up very slowly, backing away as the puppy watched.

"Come on," Lara whispered, standing up, too. "Come on, puppy. Amelia's got more cheese. Yummy cheese. Come on."

Amelia held out the foil—there were still five or six pieces of cheese left—and the two girls retreated slowly up the alley.

"Don't stare at him," Lara whispered. "He came out from the garbage cans when we were looking in our bags, didn't he? I don't think dogs like it when you stare at them—it makes them think you're scary."

"Okay." Amelia nodded. "But it's hard not to. Is he following us?"

Lara looked back, keeping her eyes down toward the ground. Even though she wasn't looking straight at the puppy, she could see little black paws trotting after them. "Yes," she whispered back. "He's coming. I think we should give him some more cheese at the end of the alley."

"Good idea." Amelia fumbled a cube of cheese out of the foil and held it behind her as they came to the road. "Oh, he tickles!"

The puppy padded after the two girls, intent on the food. But as they came out of the alley and onto the pavement, he stopped, crouching back against the wall. He didn't want to go this way—the cars were loud, and there were people hurrying past. He felt safe in the alley and the leafy bushes behind the fence.

But there was food, so close. The two girls had soft voices, and they weren't very big. He could smell the cheese that one of them was holding out for him, just a little way along the pavement.

Nervously, he scurried after Lara and Amelia and took another cube of cheese—and another, and another, as they walked him home.

Chapter Four
Somewhere Safe

"I'm going to shut the gate," Lara whispered. "Do you have any cheese left?"

"Just one piece," Amelia whispered back. "But I bet I can keep him sniffing the foil for a while." She crouched down by Lara's front door and held out the last piece of cheese while Lara gently pushed the front gate shut. The puppy scarfed the cheese and then licked her hand thoroughly. Amelia opened the foil and held it in front of his nose. Lara was just about to sneak around them and ring the doorbell when she heard a thud from inside the house, then a scratching of claws and an excited woof.

Oliver! He'd heard them outside his front door. Lara looked back at the puppy just as he reversed suddenly out of the foil, his ears flattening. She could tell he was going to run —and there were loose boards in the fence, even though the gate was shut.

Lara only thought for a split second— Dad had said to be careful in case the stray dog was scared and snapped at her, but the puppy had been so gentle eating her sandwich and the cheese. She slipped

53

her hands around his bony ribcage and picked him up, cradling him against her jacket.

"Lara!" Amelia hissed. "Be careful!"

"I am. It's okay, it's okay. Shh."

The puppy seemed to have frozen. As the front door opened and Dad and Oliver appeared, Lara could feel him shaking. But he didn't try to bite or struggle.

Dad looked at her and then down at Oliver, who was wagging his tail and making little whining noises as if he'd never seen anything so exciting. Quickly, he scooted Oliver back into the house— Lara guessed he was shutting him in the kitchen—and then he appeared in the doorway again. He didn't look as happy as Lara had thought he would.

"We found the puppy," she said hopefully.

"You went off on your own looking for a stray dog," her dad said, trying to keep his voice gentle. "That was really not a good idea."

"But we rescued him!" Lara protested, and she felt the puppy wriggle in her arms as he heard her voice rise.

"Shh…. Try not to scare him, Lara,"

Dad said. "Come on, you'd better bring him inside."

"What about Oliver?"

"I put him in the backyard."

The girls followed Lara's dad into the house, and Amelia quickly shut the front door behind them. The puppy whined anxiously at the bang, and Lara shushed him as gently as she could.

"It was my idea, too," Amelia told Lara's dad as they entered the kitchen and Lara set the puppy down on the floor. "I wanted to see him—and then we thought of our leftover lunches."

"But what if he'd bitten you? Girls, you don't know anything about him! I know he doesn't look fierce, but you just can't tell."

"Dad, please can you sit down on the

floor or … or go over there behind the table? Please? It's just I think you're scaring him—you're too big!"

"What? Oh…." Lara's dad looked down at the puppy, who was pressing himself as tightly as he could against Lara's knees. The little dog had his tail tucked right between his legs, and his eyes were closed—if he couldn't see the scary man, maybe the scary man wasn't there….

"I'm sorry, Dad."

"It's okay." Lara's dad backed away a little and then sat down on the kitchen floor. "But dogs can get jumpy when they're scared. You two really shouldn't have tried to bring him home. He could have hurt you."

"Aren't you glad we found him?" Lara

asked. The puppy was looking sideways at Lara's dad, still scared, but he'd relaxed a little now that the big man wasn't looming over him.

Dad sighed. "Yes, of course I am! You know I was worried about him out there on his own. But even though he's tiny, he can still bite."

"I'm sorry, Dad," Lara whispered again.

"I'm sorry, too, Mr. Fisher," Amelia said, looking guilty. "He didn't ever snap at us, though."

There was a sudden scratching at the back door, and Dad shook his head. "Oliver knows that something's going on. We can't keep him out there forever."

"He didn't bark at the puppy when we saw him in the alley," Lara pointed out.

"I'm not worried about Oliver," Dad said. "He likes other dogs. But we don't know how this one's going to react."

Oliver scratched at the door again, and Amelia squeaked. "It's open!"

"What?" Dad tried to get up from the floor, but he wasn't quick enough. Oliver came nosing curiously around the door, his tail waving when he saw them all sitting on the floor. It looked like a game—he liked being able to bounce on top of people.

"Gently, Oliver," Dad said, reaching out to grab his collar. "I guess I didn't shut the door all the way. I was in a hurry...."

Oliver stood next to Dad, peering at the puppy, his ears pricked up. Lara thought he looked friendly, but she wasn't sure what Oliver looked like to the smaller dog. An enormous frightening thing, maybe?

As if he understood what she was thinking, Oliver crouched down, settling onto the floor with his nose on his long front paws. He lay there quietly, snuffling at the puppy.

"It's okay," Lara whispered to the puppy. "Oliver's friendly. He likes you."

Oliver gave a huge yawn and got up, wandering away to his water bowl. He didn't seem to mind that there was another dog in his house.

The puppy watched him go and thumped his tail against Lara's leg. Then he licked her knee and looked up at her. Lara rubbed his head and his tail wagged again, just a little.

"That was good," Dad said quietly. "Oliver's not taking too much notice, and this little one is pretty calm." He sighed. "I guess we'd better hold on to him until tomorrow, and then I'll take him to the rescue center. I'll call animal control and let her know we've got him, too."

"Won't they want to take him right away?" Lara asked sadly. She and Amelia were both petting the puppy now and the little dog seemed to like it, nuzzling gently at their hands.

"No, when I spoke to her before, she said they take any stray dogs to Valley Animal Care. So we can just drop him off there tomorrow."

Lara sighed. Poor little dog. She knew he'd be well taken care of at the rescue center, but he deserved to have a real home. Like Oliver did. A home like theirs.

The puppy followed Lara and Amelia into the yard, sniffing curiously at Oliver's basket as he went past. The big dog was curled up in there, watching him. The puppy gave him a hopeful

62

look—was the big dog friendly?

Another dog had come sniffing around the alley a few days before and the puppy had approached him, remembering his mother and the other puppies. He remembered playing and wrestling with them, and sleeping snuggled up together. He'd hoped the dog might help him find some food. Instead, it had snarled at him and then snapped angrily. The puppy had retreated through the fence and hidden away under the bushes, trembling. He wasn't sure if this big dog would snap, too....

But as the puppy ran after the two girls, the big dog wandered out into the yard and sniffed at him gently. When the girl who had picked him up rolled a ball toward them, the puppy nosed at it doubtfully. He'd never played with a ball, and he wasn't sure what to do with it. He looked up at the big dog and watched curiously as he nudged the ball and flipped it up into the air with his nose. The ball landed just in front of the puppy's paws, and he yapped excitedly. The big dog seemed to be waiting for him to do something....

The puppy ran at the ball, meaning to push it with his nose as the big dog had done. But he didn't get it quite right— his paws hit the ball first and he rolled over with it, tumbling in the grass as the girls giggled behind him. He gave the ball a confused look. What had happened?

The big dog leaned down and licked

the puppy's nose. The little dog liked that. It felt good. He stumbled up and followed the big dog as he ambled back into the house, keeping close by its long legs. The puppy clambered over the doorstep, and the big dog looked back at him patiently. The two girls and the man were watching, and the puppy scuttled nervously across the floor toward the big dog, who was slumping down in his basket again.

The puppy wasn't quite brave enough to climb in with him, so he sat next to the basket instead, watching as the two girls came to sit down at the kitchen table. Then the big dog leaned over and licked him again, the huge tongue pulling his ears back. His mother had licked him like that, the puppy remembered.

Slowly, he eased himself down so that he was lying on the floor with just his nose resting next to the big dog's paws. He still didn't know what had happened to his mother and the other puppies—all he could remember was scratching his way out of a cardboard box and finding himself in the alley. But for the first time in a long time, someone was taking care of him. He was somewhere safe.

Chapter Five
A Rough Night

"You should give him a name," Amelia said. "You can't just keep calling him 'puppy.'" Lara's dad had gotten them a drink and left them to keep an eye on the puppy while he called animal control.

"I know," Lara said, leaning around the edge of the table to look at the little dog, who was still curled up next to Oliver. "I keep thinking of awesome names. But Dad's going to take him to the rescue center tomorrow. And if I give him a name, it'll make saying good-bye to him even harder." She looked back at Amelia and lowered her voice so that her dad wouldn't hear her from the living room. "I wish we could keep him, but I don't think Dad would say yes."

Amelia smiled. "You should definitely keep him! I'm sure you could persuade your dad."

"Yeah … I guess I could try."

Amelia glanced at the clock. "Oh, wow, it's four-thirty. I wish I could stay, but my cousins are coming over, so Mom said not to be at yours for too long." She got up quietly, trying not to disturb the two dogs. "'Bye, little one."

"Are you leaving, Amelia?" Lara's dad came back, holding his phone. "Lara, I told animal control that I'll take the puppy to the rescue center tomorrow."

Amelia gave Lara a meaningful look as they went to the front door, and Lara sighed. It was easy for Amelia to say they should keep the puppy. She wasn't the one who had to persuade her dad! But still....

"Jet," Lara said as Amelia fiddled with the gate.

Amelia turned back to look at her. "Oooh! Nice name!"

"I know. He's almost all black, and if I brushed him, I bet his coat would be really shiny."

Amelia ran back up the path and gave Lara a hug. "You have to keep him! Ask your dad now!"

Lara went slowly back into the house, trying to think about what to say. Her dad was making a cup of tea, and the puppy had gotten up and was wandering around the kitchen, sniffing thoughtfully at the cupboards. Lara went to lean against the counter next to her dad.

"Do you think ... maybe ... we could keep him?" she blurted out.

Her dad laughed. "I was wondering how long that would take."

"But he's so sweet! And Oliver likes him."

"We don't want two dogs."

"I do!"

Her dad sighed. "I can see that."

"Oliver would love having company

while you're working," Lara pointed out. Her dad worked from home, and Oliver would lie behind his chair looking mournful and hoping for walks.

"Mmm. Maybe."

"I don't think it would be any more work having two dogs instead of one." Lara put her arms around her dad's waist and hugged him. "I don't want him to go to the rescue center, Dad. He seems really shy. I think he'd hate it there."

"I know. I just never planned on having more than one dog...." Lara's dad looked down at her. "I'll think about it, okay?"

"Yes!"

"I'm not promising anything, Lara...."

Even though Dad kept telling her not to get her hopes up, Lara couldn't help it. Jet was so sweet, and he seemed to get along really well with Oliver. And he was almost house-trained. Well, he might have made a puddle on the kitchen floor, but only because Lara hadn't realized in time that he wanted to go out. He was losing his nervousness around her dad, too. He actually sat next to his chair during dinner, and Lara was sure that Dad was happy, even though he said the puppy was just hoping for some hamburger.

Lara hadn't meant to call the puppy Jet in front of Dad but it slipped out, and Dad agreed it was a great name for him. Lara was sure he wouldn't have said that if he didn't want to keep the little dog, would he?

"I think I'll take Oliver upstairs to sleep in my room tonight," Dad said as Lara was saying good night. "Then we can let Jet stay in the kitchen. I don't want to leave the two of them alone together overnight, just in case."

"They'd be okay!" Lara protested.

"Probably," Dad agreed. "But I don't

want to take the chance. They've only known each other a few hours. We're just being sensible."

Lara nodded. "I guess you're used to sleeping on your own, aren't you," she said, tickling Jet under his silky chin. It was the only part of him that wasn't black—a perfect little white splotch down his front. The puppy closed his eyes blissfully, and one of his back paws tapped against the floor over and over.

Dad laughed. "You've found his perfect scratching spot. But it's bedtime now. Sleep well, sweetheart. Don't worry, I'll take care of him. And I'll make sure he goes out in the yard before I go to bed."

"'Night, Dad. And ... thank you!"

"I'm still not promising!"

Lara hurried upstairs, thinking that she was going to behave perfectly, just in case. No reading with a flashlight under the covers tonight. She curled up in bed, imagining Jet in Oliver's basket downstairs. She smiled to herself, thinking of the tiny black dog in the middle of that huge basket.

She wasn't sure what time it was when she woke up—her heart was thumping, and she'd been having a strange dream about … about … she wasn't sure what, but it had been scary, and someone was crying.

Then the crying came again, from downstairs.

Jet! She must have heard him whining, and the noise had become

75

part of her dream. Lara slipped out of bed and hurried downstairs as the pitiful cries grew louder.

Jet scratched at the kitchen door when he heard footsteps. Someone was coming! They had to let him out. He'd been dozing, but he couldn't settle down in that big basket. He needed to get back to his place—the alley and the garbage cans and the pile of old cardboard boxes. He knew that space. He was safe there. Here, everything was strange.

As the door opened, he shot through the gap and raced along the hallway, still whining. Then he sat down by the locked front door and began to howl. He wanted to go home!

But Lara came hurrying after him, whispering gently, and the man was coming down the stairs, too. Jet whimpered. He couldn't get out of here, and he wasn't even sure why he wanted to. Not when there was food and a warm bed and people who patted him and spoke gently to him and scratched his ears. Things just ... weren't right.

"Hey, shh. It's okay. Come on." Lara coaxed him along the hallway and Jet followed her wearily, settling back into the basket. She wrapped the blanket over him, shushed him again, and then crept away. Jet watched the kitchen door close behind them, the thin bar of light shrinking away to nothing, and he tried to sleep.

"Do you think he'll be okay?" Lara asked Dad worriedly as they went back upstairs.

"He's just getting used to a new place. Go to bed, sweetheart, or you'll be tired in the morning. 'Night."

Lara wrapped her comforter around herself, trying to listen for noises downstairs—there were a couple of whimpers, but that was all. Maybe Dad was right, and Jet just needed to get used to the kitchen. She rolled over and fell asleep again almost at once.

This time, she dreamed she was hurrying down the stairs to Jet, but she couldn't get there—the stairs seemed to go on and on forever, and he kept on crying. She woke up with a gasp and almost screamed as Oliver licked her hand.

"What are you doing?" she whispered, patting him. "I thought you were sleeping in Dad's room. Oh...." She could hear it now—sad little whining noises from downstairs. "Did Jet wake you up?" She climbed out of bed, more slowly and sleepily this time, and stumbled down the stairs to the kitchen with Oliver loping after her.

"Oh, Jet. Can't you sleep?" she whispered. This time the puppy didn't shoot out the door. He just crept toward her beating his tail, looking miserable and somehow as though he was saying sorry. "It's okay. It's weird being in a new place. It took me a long time to get used to my room at Mom and Jake's house."

Lara yawned and sat down next to the basket. It was nice and warm here by the radiator. "In you go," she said, patting the cushion in the bottom. The puppy looked uncertainly at Oliver, but the bigger dog climbed in first and leaned his head over the side to rest on Lara's knee. Jet followed him, snuggling up on top of Oliver's paws, and closed his eyes.

Chapter Six
The Surprise

"Lara! Have you been here all night?"

Lara blinked sleepily at her dad and then looked around in surprise. She was still sitting on the kitchen floor, huddled against the radiator. She was chilly and stiff … but there was a little black dog snuggled up asleep in her lap.

"Oh—he was in the basket before. He went to sleep on me!" she whispered, her eyes shining.

"Yes." Dad sighed. "But he didn't go to sleep in the basket by himself, which is what we were hoping for.... I'm exhausted, and I bet you are, too."

Lara didn't say anything. It wouldn't be a good idea to tell Dad that Jet falling asleep in her lap was just about the nicest thing that could have happened. At least not right now....

"You'd better go and get ready for school," Dad said. "Hello, pup," he added as Jet opened one eye and peered up at him. "Come on. Do you want to go out in the yard?"

Oliver surged up out of his basket as Dad unlocked the back door, and the two dogs headed outside together. Dad and Lara stood by the door staring after them, smiling.

"They get along really well…," Lara pointed out.

"I know. Go and get ready for school!"

Jet sat adoringly by Dad's feet while they were eating their toast for breakfast, and Lara could tell Dad liked it.

"Can Jet come to school with us?" she asked hopefully as she put on her jacket. If Dad was still set on taking the puppy to the rescue center today, this would be the last time she'd see him. She didn't want to say good-bye to him just yet.

Dad looked thoughtful. "I'm not sure. I don't think he's used to a collar and leash. But I don't want to leave him on his own, and it's probably not a good idea to leave him and Oliver together…. Yes, okay, then. We've got Oliver's old collar somewhere, and it should just about fit."

"It's in here, I'm sure it is." Lara dug around in the basket of gloves and scarves and other random things that lived under the coat hooks. "Here!" She handed the battered old collar to

Dad and held Jet, who was trying to climb into the basket, too. The puppy shook his ears, confused, as Dad fastened the collar around his neck. He gave the leash to Lara. "Be careful, okay? If he pulls a lot, I'll take him."

Lara nodded, biting her lip. It felt as if Jet was really theirs … but he wasn't.

"I get the feeling I'm going to end up carrying him," Dad muttered, but Jet didn't seem to mind the collar as they headed down the path and out of the gate. He pulled a little, but he was happy to follow Dad and Oliver, and his tail was wagging.

Lara gave Dad an anxious look as they came to the alley, wondering if the puppy would try to dash off down there. Dad put a hand on Jet's leash, too, just in case. But Jet just stopped and looked down it, his ears twitching. Oliver circled back and sniffed at him and the puppy set  off again, as if it meant nothing at all.

Lara walked proudly up to the school gate with Jet, then gave his leash to Dad and crouched down to pat him and say good-bye. "You were so good!" she whispered. "'Bye, Jet. 'Bye, handsome." She looked up at Dad with a pleading look on her face.

"Two dogs, Lara. It's a lot of work. Especially if he's not going to settle down at night." But even as he said it, Dad was tickling Jet behind the ears and smiling.

"You brought him with you!" Amelia came hurrying up beside them. "Oh, he looks so cute in a collar and leash! Are you going to keep him?"

Dad sighed, and Lara shook her head. "I don't think so. Come on." She grabbed Amelia's arm and hurried into school without looking back. She didn't want to see Jet and Oliver and Dad watching her.

"It won't be like he's a stray again," Amelia pointed out. "They'll feed him at the rescue center and make a fuss of him. He won't be hungry anymore."

"Yeah." Lara nodded firmly. "He'll probably really like it there." They'd been talking about Jet on and off all day, and Amelia had been doing a great job of cheering Lara up. It was sort of working…. "It's going to be weird walking past the alley, though," she added as she slung her backpack over her shoulder and they headed for the door. "I don't think I'll ever be able to walk past it without checking for a puppy now."

"I know! Hey—your dad's here. I thought we were walking back on our own."

"We were." Lara caught her breath. "Do you think…. Yes! Look!"

Dad was there, just outside the gate, with Oliver sitting patiently beside him. And next to them—dancing around and tying himself in knots with Oliver's old leash—was Jet.

"You didn't take him to the rescue center!" Lara yelled as she dashed toward her dad. "Are we keeping him?" She bent down to pet Jet, and he bounced up at her lovingly. He was trying to lick her nose and wag his tail and say hello to Amelia

all at the same time. Already he seemed so different from the scared little dog they'd found the day before.

Dad grinned at her. "I called Valley Animal Care, but the lady I spoke to sounded a little worried about where they'd put him. She said they were really full. So ... I thought we'd try keeping him a little longer. He's been so good today. He went on a long walk with me and Oliver at lunchtime, and then he fell asleep on my foot while I was working."

"You see! You love him!" Lara said triumphantly, and Amelia laughed.

Dad held out Jet's leash and Lara took it, then she offered it to Amelia. "Do you want a turn walking him?"

Amelia took the leash, beaming,

and they set off down the road. Lara saw quite a few people smiling at the two dogs as they went past—Oliver was so big that he made Jet look even littler.

"We just have to hope he settles down better tonight," Dad said.

Lara nodded. "I know. Maybe he could sleep in my room?"

"Oh, you're so lucky," Amelia sighed enviously.

But Dad shook his head. "I'm sorry, Lara. He's not totally house-trained, and your room has carpet. He needs to stay downstairs where there are hard floors."

"I guess," Lara said reluctantly.

"But maybe both he and Oliver could be in the kitchen tonight," Dad suggested. "They seem to be getting along really well. Hopefully that'll help."

"We could put Oliver's upstairs basket in the kitchen, too, in case they each want a bed," Lara agreed, smiling at Jet as he walked along beside Amelia. She couldn't believe how good he was being.

"I hope it goes okay with him tonight," Amelia said, handing Jet's leash back as they reached her front door. "He's such a good dog. I bet it was just first-night nerves or something."

Lara smiled at her. "I'll tell you tomorrow!"

At bedtime, Lara carried Oliver's spare basket downstairs, and then hurried back up for an armful of soft toys.

"What are those for?" Dad asked as she brought them into the kitchen.

"I thought we could make the basket feel a little smaller," Lara explained. "It's so big, and Jet's so little. If we put these around the edge, it won't seem so big to him."

"Good idea," Dad agreed. "I hope none are your favorites, though. He might eat them...."

Lara shook her head. "No. They're just the ones that live in the box under my bed." She started to line up the toys around the inside of the basket so there was just a little Jet-sized space in the middle. The puppy stood next to her, peering in curiously. When she'd finished, he climbed into the basket and sat down, surrounded by teddy bears. A couple of them were bigger than he was.

"There!" Lara smiled. "You'll be cozy now. Sleep well, Jet."

Dad laughed. "I think Oliver's jealous. He wants a bear, too."

Lara dashed upstairs and came back with an old toy dog, and Oliver snuggled down with it tucked under his chin. She went up to bed feeling hopeful—both dogs looked so comfy with their baskets next to each other and all those toys.

But in the middle of the night, she and Dad were woken by a miserable howl.

Dad was already heading downstairs when Lara came out of her room. "Go back to sleep, sweetheart. You don't need to get up."

But Lara followed Dad anyway. She couldn't leave Jet making such sad noises. The puppy was waiting by the kitchen door again, whimpering. As Dad opened the door, he tried to wriggle past them and dash along the hallway to the front door.

"What is it, Jet?" Dad asked, picking up the puppy and gently rubbing his back. "Are you scared?"

Jet whined again, and Oliver made a sleepy sort of groaning noise. "I know," Dad muttered. "I feel the same way. Come on, pup. Bedtime." Carefully he put Jet back into the basket. Lara tucked the toys around him again, and then they crept out of the kitchen.

The sad whimpering started when they were halfway up the stairs, and every so often there was a little howl. Dad sighed. "I think we have to try leaving him. It's no good if he thinks that we're going to come and make a fuss of him every time he cries."

"But he's so sad." Lara peered over the banisters. The noises were making her feel awful.

"You can't sleep in the kitchen with him every night," Dad said firmly. "Come on, Lara. You're just going to have to put your comforter over your head." He frowned. "I hope he isn't going to wake up the people next door...."

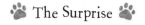

In the kitchen Jet sat by the door, scratching at it with one paw. Why had they gone and left him again? Oliver was there—he was asleep. Jet could hear the big dog's soft breathing in the darkness. Oliver must feel safe here, safe enough to sleep. But somehow this place wasn't right. It was too big. Too … different.

Jet scratched the door again and let out a desperate wail. There was dark all around him, and it was all too cold and open and empty. When Lara was there, patting him, he wasn't so scared, but he hated being alone. He howled again, and again, and again….

Chapter Seven
Another Sleepless Night

Dad was looking very tired and grumpy the next morning. Jet had gone to sleep eventually, but he seemed to have been crying forever. Even Oliver looked tired—he didn't leap out of his basket as soon as his dog biscuits hit the food bowl the way he usually did.

"That was not a good night," Dad said grimly.

"No." Lara stirred her cereal and looked hopefully at him. "It's such a big change for him, Dad. Babies take a long time to sleep through the night. Mom said I was awful at sleeping when I was little."

"Don't remind me." Dad shuddered. "At least he isn't that bad."

"So ... we'll try again tonight? I could call Mom and ask if she knows how to help a dog sleep."

Dad nodded. "He has to settle down soon. You're right—he just needs to get used to us."

Lara spent the rest of the day trying to think of clever ways to help Jet sleep.

"Maybe he'd like a hot-water bottle," her friend Jackson suggested at lunch. Lara and Amelia had told most of the class about Jet by now. "We gave our cat a hot-water bottle when we first got her. My mom said it was to remind Furball of sleeping next to her mom."

"He didn't have his mom when he was sleeping by the garbage cans, though," Amelia pointed out.

"I'm going to try everything," Lara said. "Oh! Do you think he'd like a night-light? Maybe he doesn't like the dark. That alley had security lights at the back of the stores."

"It's a worth a try," Jackson agreed. "He's a really cute dog. I'd love a dog like that."

"He looks beautiful now that I've brushed him," Lara said. "He's all sleek and shiny. He just needs to gain a little weight, but he's eating a lot, so hopefully he won't be too thin for very long."

Amelia was staying for art club, so Dad, Oliver, and Jet came to pick Lara up. Jet already looked less like a stray, Lara realized when she saw him sitting by the gate. She was sure it wasn't as easy to see his ribs as it had been before.

"I've got some ideas for helping Jet sleep," she told her dad. "Jackson thinks we should give him a hot-water bottle, but I'm not sure about that. What if he eats it? He'll get all wet, and he definitely won't sleep then."

"It might not be worth the risk," Dad agreed.

"But I've got another idea that's awesome. I'll show you when we get home."

Lara dashed upstairs when they got in, then came down holding her old owl night-light. It glowed a soft golden color, and she'd loved it when she was little. It had been standing on her bookcase for years.

"I think there were lights on in the alley," she explained to Dad. "Maybe Jet's just not used to sleeping in the dark...."

Dad popped his head around the door to check on Lara when he went to bed that night, and she turned over to look at him. "Is Jet okay?" she asked sleepily.

"Seems to be. Not a sound. Maybe the night-light was the answer! Mom said it sounded like a good idea."

"Yay...." Lara closed her eyes again. She was so tired after two nights of lousy sleep that she felt like she could sleep forever.

But a little while later, she woke up. Was that Jet? Or had she just dreamed it? No.... She sighed. There were definite whimpers coming from downstairs.

Dad had said just to leave him if she heard him, but Lara wasn't sure she could. The puppy sounded so sad. Besides, she really didn't want him to wake Dad. If Jet wouldn't sleep properly, Dad might give up on him and say he had to go to the rescue center after all. Lara was sure he just needed a little more time.

She hurried downstairs as quietly as she could and let herself into the kitchen. There was Jet by the door again, this time lit by the soft glow of the night-light. "What's the matter, sweetie pie?" she whispered, shutting the door. "Come on, back in your basket. Hey, Oliver." She made a fuss of the big dog, too, and Oliver snorted and tucked his nose back under his tail.

"Didn't the night-light help?" Lara whispered to Jet as she settled down next to the radiator again. She giggled wearily as he climbed into her lap. "What are we going to do with you?" she muttered. "I can't go to sleep down here. Dad'll be upset...." But she couldn't help it. She was just too tired to keep her eyes open.

When she woke up, it was getting light, and Jet was a saggy ball of black fur in her lap. Lara looked anxiously at the clock on the oven—there was half an hour until she usually got up. If she could sneak back upstairs without waking Dad, maybe he'd think Jet had slept by himself. She didn't want to lie—but she didn't want Dad to send Jet away, either.

"Are you okay?" Amelia nudged Lara gently. Lara jumped awake and pushed her glasses back up. "Were you asleep? Come on, Lara, it's math. You've only done one question."

"I'm sorry," Lara whispered. "I slept in the kitchen with Jet again last night. I'm really tired. I pretended to Dad that he'd slept on his own, though." She smothered a huge yawn behind her hand.

Amelia understood. "Was he happy?"

"Yes, but I felt awful when he kept saying how great it was...." Lara sighed.

"Get going with your math, please, you two." Miss Okafor smiled at them.

"No talking."

Lara nodded, but it was hard to concentrate on fractions when she felt so sleepy. And it got worse as the day went on. Even the fresh air outside at lunch didn't help. She felt like lying down on one of the playground benches for a nap.

She just about managed to stay awake through the afternoon, but a couple of times she saw Miss Okafor watching her. At least it was Friday. She'd have the weekend to relax and catch up on sleep.

Only another fifteen minutes, Lara told herself as Miss Okafor picked up the book she was reading to the class. I can stay awake for that. But even though she was loving the story, it was just so soothing being read to. Lara's eyes kept closing, and a couple of times, Amelia had to kick her under the table. When the bell rang for the end of school, Lara sat up suddenly and saw that Amelia was making worried faces at her.

"I tried to get you to wake up, but you wouldn't!" she whispered as they gathered up their stuff.

"Lara!"

Lara turned and looked guiltily at their teacher. "Yes?"

"Can you come with me a minute, please? I just want to have a word with your dad. You can go on, Amelia. Have a good weekend."

Lara sighed and shuffled after Miss Okafor. Her teacher had definitely seen that she'd been asleep. "My dad will be just outside the gate," Lara explained.

"He's got our dogs with him, so he can't come into the playground."

"Okay." Miss Okafor led the way to the gate. Lara felt like everyone in the playground was watching them and wondering what she'd done.

Dad looked anxiously at Lara as he saw them coming. "Is there a problem?" he asked.

Miss Okafor smiled. "I just wanted to know if Lara's having trouble sleeping. She seemed very tired today. She actually fell asleep in class just now."

"Oh…." Dad groaned. "I'm really sorry. We've had a couple of sleepless nights." He held up Jet's leash. "We've accidentally got another dog—he was a stray. Lara found him."

"He's beautiful." Miss Okafor smiled

111

at Lara. "Lucky you!"

Dad smiled. "Yes, he's great. But he's still getting used to us, and he's been waking up during the night a lot. Last night was better though, I thought." Dad looked at Lara, and Lara looked down at her feet. "Well, thanks for mentioning it. I'll make sure that Lara gets plenty of sleep this weekend. Come on, sweetheart. We'd better head home."

Lara followed her dad down the road, still looking at her feet instead of looking at him. She was pretty sure he was waiting for her to say something, but she didn't know how to start.

"Did you go downstairs last night after all?" Dad asked eventually. "Did Jet wake up?"

"Yes," Lara admitted.

"How long were you downstairs with him?"

"Um. A long time…."

"Oh, Lara. Did you sleep there again?"

"He was so lonely, Dad," Lara sniffed.

Dad shook his head. "I don't think this is going to work, Lara. You can't sleep with Jet every night! I can't believe I didn't wake up—and you let me think he slept through the night."

"I'm sorry! I just didn't want you to be upset with him." Lara's voice shook. "I thought you might say he had to go to the rescue center. And I was right, because now you are!"

"I'm sorry, sweetheart. I just don't think we can cope with him not sleeping. You've got to be awake for school."

"But he'll hate it there!" Lara stopped

113

and crouched down to rub Jet's ears and the smooth fur on the top of his head. He was watching her with dark, anxious eyes. "Look how beautiful he is now that he's eating properly. He loves us, and he loves Oliver. We can't get rid of him."

"They're wonderful at taking care of dogs at the rescue center," Dad said gently. "They'll probably know what to do to help him sleep. And he'll have a perfect home soon—he's such a sweet puppy, Lara. Someone will want him."

Lara looked up at her dad with eyes full of tears. "*I* want him!"

Chapter Eight
The Perfect Solution

Dad had arranged to call someone for work, but he said they'd take Jet to the rescue center when he was done. Lara couldn't even answer him—not without starting to cry. As soon as they got home, she took Jet out into the yard. She got Oliver's grooming brush from the kitchen drawer on the way and sat down with the puppy held between her knees. Oliver followed her out and lay down next to her with his head on his paws.

"I know you're still a little thin," she said to Jet. "But you're going to look beautiful. I don't want them thinking you aren't special." She ran the brush gently down his back, and he wriggled delightedly. He loved being brushed.

"I wish we could figure out why you can't sleep," Lara whispered to him. "I know you like living with us. You're so friendly. You love Oliver." She smiled as the greyhound heard his name and lifted his head to look at her. "And I think you love me and Dad." Her voice wobbled again. "So what's the problem?"

She laid down the brush, and Jet climbed onto her knees and nuzzled at her chin. "I can't believe it was better sleeping outside by those garbage cans than it is living in our house," Lara said as he tried to lick her ears. She caught hold of his front paws gently and stared at him. "What is it that's wrong with here? Whenever you wake us up, you're always desperate to get out the front door. You want to go back there, don't you?" She shook her head. "I just don't understand. But ... maybe you could show me. Stay here a minute."

Lara crept back inside. Dad was still

in his office, talking on the phone. She had a little while, she figured. She grabbed Jet's leash off the hook in the hall and went back into the yard. Oliver got up, tail waving happily, and Lara patted him and smoothed his ears. "I can't take you out right now, okay? There's something I have to do with Jet. But it's the weekend, and I promise you'll get a really good walk tomorrow, a long one."

Oliver stared mournfully after them as they slipped out the side gate and around the house.

"Come on," Lara muttered as Jet bounced happily along the pavement. "Show me."

When they got to the alley, she stopped and let Jet lead her. He sniffed at the broken paved surface and the weeds growing at the edge of the wall, and then he looked up at her.

"Yes, I know. We're back," Lara crouched down and tickled under his chin. "There's something here, isn't there?" She looked over at the garbage cans at the end of the alley, suddenly wondering if another puppy would peer out between them. Maybe that was why Jet wanted to go back—maybe he had a brother or a sister abandoned out here, too.

Then she shook her head. If Jet wanted to find another puppy, he'd be desperate to get out of the house all the time. But he only seemed to want to go back at night. When they walked past the alley on the way to or from school, he wasn't that bothered. Lara sighed. "Is it that you like sleeping outside?" she wondered.

Jet didn't even hear her. He was stomping eagerly toward the garbage cans and the pile of scruffy cardboard boxes next to them. He tugged at his leash, pulling Lara after him, and put his nose down to the ground, sniffing his way all around his old home. There was no food lying around, but that didn't matter. He wasn't hungry—or he was only a little hungry because he hadn't had his dinner yet. It was a strange feeling, not to be desperate to eat.

But he was tired. He felt as though he hadn't slept well for days and days. He needed a little space to curl up in, somewhere he felt safe. The basket and the big kitchen and the house just weren't right. He poked his nose into several of the cardboard boxes, trying to find one that was dry and clean— and there it was. The perfect box. Just a little bigger than he was. Not too damp. And it smelled good—like cookies.

Jet crawled inside the box and curled up, not minding that he had his leash wrapped around his legs. This was exactly what he'd been looking for.

He was asleep in seconds.

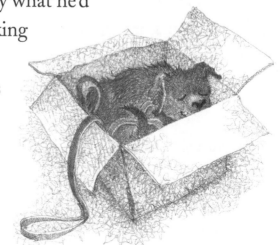

"Lara!"

Lara looked around guiltily. Dad hadn't known where she was. "I'm sorry…. But Dad, look."

"You can't go off on your own like that! I thought you were in the yard, and then Oliver came and found me and I realized you were gone." Her dad looked around. "Lara, did you let Jet go? Are you trying to stop me from taking him to the rescue center?"

"No!" Lara shook her head. "I wouldn't do that. I know the rescue center is better than him being a stray. But I don't think we need to take him there after all." She moved over so that Dad could see better. "Look. He's asleep."

Lara's dad squatted down next to her and looked into the box. Oliver looked in, too, sniffing gently at the sleeping puppy.

"A box?" Dad frowned.

"He just got right in and went to sleep. Like it was exactly what he needed." Lara gazed up hopefully at Dad. "If he always slept in a box out here, maybe he doesn't feel right sleeping in a basket."

"It does make sense," Dad said slowly. "It's worth a try, anyway. Here, you take Oliver's leash." He handed it to Lara and then reached down to slip his hands under Jet's box. The puppy shifted a little as the box wobbled, but he didn't wake up. Dad laughed. "He seems pretty happy," he said. "Not sure about this box, though, Lara. It doesn't look like it's going to last long."

"We could get some more. I can go

and ask at the convenience store," Lara suggested. "I bet they have some."

"Good idea," Dad agreed, then shifted the box so he had it in one arm and put his other arm around Lara. "Looks like we're going to need them...."

The box that Jet had chosen was next to Oliver's basket, but it was looking a little saggy, like it might collapse in the middle of the night. So just before she went to bed, Lara got a couple of the new ones she'd gotten from the store and lined them up, too.

"I wonder which one he'll choose," Dad said, grinning. "Hey, Oliver, they're not for you!"

Oliver was inspecting the boxes thoughtfully, sniffing and nudging them with his nose. At last he climbed into the largest one, turned around twice, and sat down. It was a tight fit for him, even sitting—then he slumped down slowly.

"You're not going to fit," Lara told him, but he looked pretty happy.

Jet had been inspecting all the boxes, too, and now he stood up with his front paws on the edge of Oliver's box, his tail wagging. Then he heaved himself over the side, flopping down on top of Oliver.

The big greyhound eyed him and seemed to sigh.

"You have a basket," Lara pointed out, trying not to laugh. "The boxes are for Jet, not you."

Jet worked himself into the tiny gap between the side of the box and Oliver's paws. From above, the entire box was full of dog—they even had corners. If Oliver twitched, Jet bounced up and down.

"Do you think they'll stay like that?" Dad whispered.

"I think so. Jet's asleep, and Oliver almost is." Lara looked up at Dad. "We figured it out."

Dad shook his head. "You did."

Lara reached in to rub Jet's head, and he half opened one eye and licked her hand. Then he went back to sleep.

HOLLY WEBB

Holly Webb started out as a children's book editor, and wrote her first series for the publisher she worked for. She has been writing ever since, with more than 100 books to her name. Holly lives in England with her husband, three children, and several cats who are always nosing around when she is trying to type on her laptop.

For more information
about Holly Webb visit:

www.holly-webb.com
www.tigertalesbooks.com